Man in the Moon

Man in the Moon

Jasmine,
Reach for the moon, and wish on
the
Stars!

written by

Kelly Young-Silverman

Kelly Yg-S.

illustrated by

erin the great

erin the great

To Evie,
the inspiration for this story.
To David,
who inspires me everyday.

-Kelly

To J.R., my moon.
To Knox, my little star.
To Kate and Kiel,
(who remind me
of the little girl in this story).

-Erin

Man in the Moon
text and illustrations copyright 2014 ©
by Kelly Young-Silverman & Erin Wicker

Published by WordCrafts Press
Tullahoma, TN 37388
www.wordcrafts.net

Man in the moon,
are you lonely up there,
Hanging down brightly
in the cold night air?

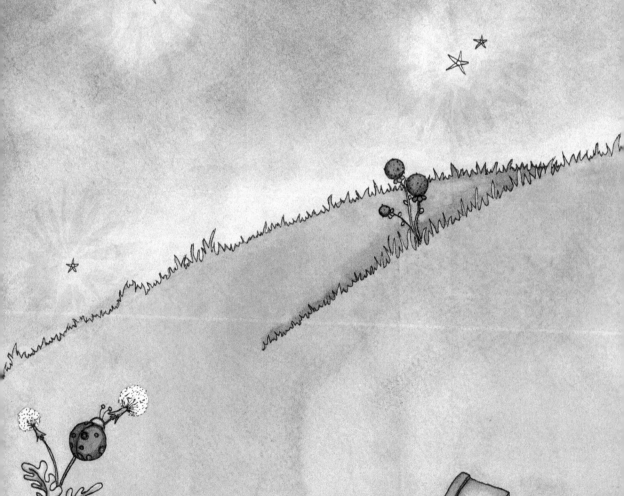

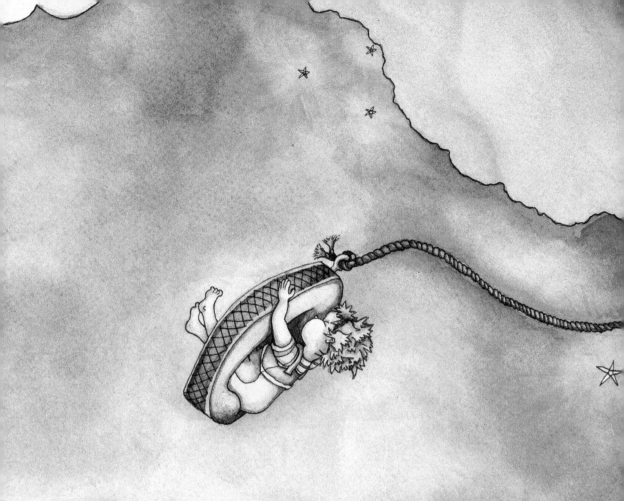

You smile so sweetly,
might I ask why?
If I were alone I think
I would cry.

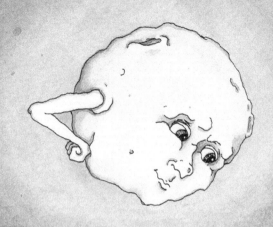

The moon says nothing,
but smiles away.
I'm not sure he heard me;
he's so far away.

So I lift my head high
and say it once more,
But this time much louder
than the time before.

Man in the moon,
are you sad in the sky?
You come only at night,
I bet you're quite shy.

For the sun is miles
away from earth, too.

And she reaches for me,
not at all like you.

The moon says nothing
but smiles away.
I bet he is laughing,
he must like
to play.

So I lift my head high
and tell him a joke.
Though I'm sure it was funny,
no word he spoke.

Man in the moon,
are you listening to me?
Or am I just too small
for the big moon to see?

Does the man in the moon
care for one little girl,
Or am I just a dot in this
great big old world?

The moon says nothing,
but smiles away.
I think now he's saying
he wants me to stay.

For though
I am only just
one little dot,
A friend is a friend,
and a friend is a lot.

So I sit up awhile
with my friend in the moon.
Then I hop into bed,
for day will come soon.

And all day tomorrow,
    I'll wait for my friend.
For ours is a friendship
    without any end!

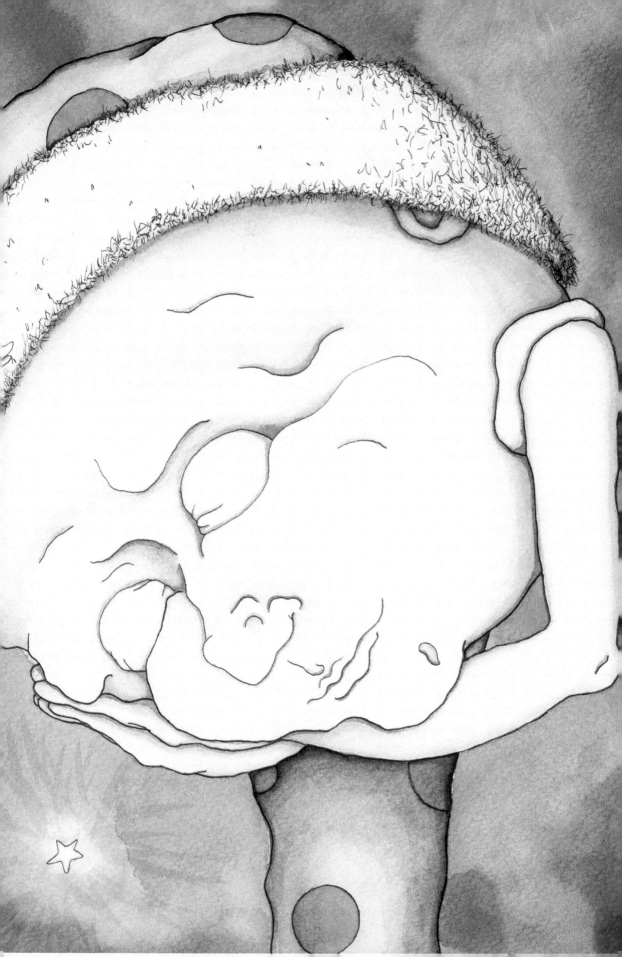

Good night, sleep tight
my little one.
The day was good,
but now it's done.

A whisper
and a good night kiss.
Sweet dreams for you,
is what I wish!

The End

CPSIA information can be obtained
at www.ICGtesting.com
Printed in the USA
LVOW05*2137291016

510852LV00010B/34/P

9 780990 976103